HENRY AND MUDGE

AND THE

Wild Wind

The Twelfth Book of Their Adventures

Story by Cynthia Rylant
Pictures by Suçie Stevenson

Ready-to-Read
Aladdin Paperbacks

To Cousin Pete—CR
For Ben Moss—SS

THE HENRY AND MUDGE BOOKS

First Aladdin Paperbacks Edition, 1996

Aladdin Paperbacks
An imprint of Simon & Schuster Children's Publishing Division
1230 Avenue of the Americas
New York, NY 10020

The text of this book was set in 18 point Goudy
The illustrations were rendered in pen-and-ink and watercolor

Manufactured in the United States of America

30 29 28 27 26 25 24 23 22 21

The Library of Congress Cataloging-in-Publication Data
Rylant, Cynthia.
Henry and Mudge and the wild wind: the twelfth book of their adventures / story by Cynthia Rylant;
pictures by Suçie Stevenson—1st ed.
p. cm.
Summary: Henry and his big dog Mudge try to keep busy inside the house during a thunderstorm.
[1. Dogs—Fiction. 2. Thunderstorms—Fiction.] 1. Stevenson, Suçie, ill. II. Title.
PZ7.R982Heb 1993
[E]—dc20 91-12644
ISBN 978-0-689-81008-4(hc.)
ISBN 978-0-689-80838-8(pbk.)
0110 LAK

Contents

Some Wind

Henry and Henry's big dog Mudge
were playing outside one hot
summer day. Suddenly the wind
blew so hard that it blew
Henry's hat away.

"Wow," said Henry. "Some wind."

Whoosh!

Mudge's fur rippled.

His ears flapped.

His eyes got all wet.

"Must be a thunderstorm coming,"
said Henry. "Uh-oh."
Henry didn't like thunderstorms.
They made him jumpy.
But they made Mudge even jumpier.

Every time a storm came,
Mudge did strange things.

He whined.
He walked around the kitchen table
about a hundred times.

He sat in the bathroom alone.

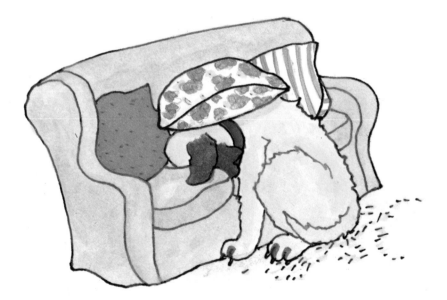

He put his head between
the couch cushions.

The only jumpy thing Henry did
was whistle a lot.
Lightning would crash and
thunder would boom and
Henry would whistle.

He whistled "Jingle Bells."

He whistled "Happy Birthday."

He even whistled "The Star-Spangled Banner" (not very well).

Henry knew what to do when
the wild wind started.
"Come on, Mudge," he said
as he headed for the house.
All at once the wind blew
open the screen door.
Crash!

Whistling and whining like crazy,
Henry and Mudge ran inside.

Pows and Booms

The sky turned very dark.

Henry's mother turned on the lights.

Henry's father shut all the windows.

Henry and Mudge sat on the couch, waiting.

Splat! Sploop!

The rain began.

Then *pow!* went the lightning.

Boom! went the thunder.

Mudge went to sit in the bathroom.

"Mudge!" Henry called.

Mudge wouldn't come back.

"Chicken," Henry grumbled.

He started whistling "Jingle Bells,"
but he missed Mudge.

Henry went to the bathroom door.

He looked at Mudge.

Mudge looked at him.

Pow! went the lightning.

"Come on, Mudge," said Henry.

"Let's go in the kitchen."

Mudge wagged his tail a little.

He followed Henry into the kitchen.

Henry's mother and Henry's father

were having cups of tea at the table.

Boom!

Mudge began to walk around the
table in a circle.

Henry began to whistle.

19

"Want some cocoa?" Henry's mother asked.

"Sure," said Henry.

Pow! went the lightning.

Henry whistled "The Star-Spangled Banner" while Mudge went around the table for the tenth time.

Henry's father and Henry's mother
just looked at each other.

The Enemy Couch

Pow!

The lights went out.

"Uh-oh," said Henry's father.

Henry switched to "Happy Birthday"

and Mudge went into the living room

to put his head in the couch.

Henry's mother brought out some candles.
Henry started the fifth round
of "Happy Birthday."
"Wait! Wait!" said Henry's father.

"Maybe you could stop whistling,"
he said to Henry, "and play a game."
Boom! went the thunder.
"What kind of game?" asked Henry.
"Uh . . . let's see," said Henry's father,
trying to think fast.
"How about the Crawling-Through-
Enemy-Lines game?" he said.

"Mudge is a prisoner in the enemy camp,"
Henry's father whispered.
"And it's your job to rescue him."
Henry looked in the living room.
Mudge still had his head in the couch.
"Uh-huh," said Henry.

Pow!

"Hear that enemy fire?" said Henry's father.

Boom!

"And that cannon?"

Henry's father's eyes were big.

Henry nodded.

He was ready to cross enemy lines.

He was ready to free Mudge

from the enemy couch.

"Don't forget to take a flashlight,"
said Henry's father.
"And watch out for scorpions."
Henry grabbed the light and
dropped to the floor.

He crawled, inch by inch,
across the enemy kitchen.
Pow! Boom!

He crawled, inch by inch,
across the enemy dining room.
Boom! Pow!

He crawled right into the enemy camp.
There was his best friend Mudge,
a bravely waiting prisoner,
with his head in the enemy couch.

"Mudge!" whispered Henry.

His brave friend lifted an ear.

"Mudge!" Henry whispered louder.

His brave friend wagged a tail.

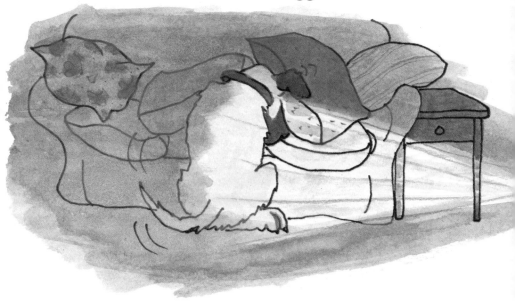

"Come on, Mudge."
Henry crawled over and pulled his
brave friend's collar.
"You're free now," Henry said.

Mudge sniffed the air of freedom.

Mudge sniffed the socks of his rescuer.

Pow! Boom!

Mudge sniffed a fast track to the bathroom.

Henry frowned.

He had hoped Mudge would stay.

"At least you missed the scorpions,"
said Henry's father.

Henry grinned a little.

"And at least you know where
to find Mudge if you need him!"
Henry's father said.

"Right!" Henry laughed.

Above Their Heads

For the rest of the storm,
Henry sat at the kitchen table
with his parents.
They played cards by candlelight.

Soon there were only little *pows*
and tiny *booms*.
Then there weren't any.
The lights came back on.
The sky cleared.
And Mudge came out of the bathroom,
wagging as if he'd been to a
cracker factory.

Henry and Mudge went back outside.

They sniffed the fresh air.

They felt the wet leaves.

And, like it was a painting,
a great, giant rainbow rose up
and spread its beautiful colors
right above their heads.